SN

Somebody, Nobody

Cristy Gerasimchuk

I'd like to dedicate this book to God, my Mom, Denis Gerasimchuk, Alfy and Vanessa Girich, and lastly, to all the people who believed in me.

My exact thoughts while writing this book;
"I'm terrified, but i've also never been more excited"

This book is about the things most of us go through, but nobody talks about.

Enjoy.

First published in 2025

Written by Cristy Gerasimchuk

ISBN 979-8-218-51775-5

Cristygerasimchuk101@gmail.com

Contents

Sunsets

train

i got stuck behind a train today
i waited many minutes for it to pass
i had my windows down
a cool breeze hitting my face
the sun was going down across a huge field
for a second i could see us
back on the train
remember how we climbed one?
in the middle of nowhere
in some small town
me and you
climbed a train
and now every time i see one
i see how happy we were
we used to be
how silly we were to climb a train
without knowing the consequences

the other day was the first time i saw you in public after you broke up with me
i saw you and immediately recognized you
i only saw you for a split second but i remember everything about it
even the clothes you were wearing
gray shirt, black shorts
you quickly opened the door and disappeared
not even looking at me
not even noticing me
but i noticed you
i think it was always like that
i hate to admit it, but i don't think you ever noticed me when we were together
all i wanted was to be noticed by the person i loved the most
but you never looked my way

i remember when you told me our relationship wouldn't change
when you promised me you'd still be around after you got married
i still remember the first time you didn't pick up my call
i remember the second
third
fourth
it wasn't even the fact that you didn't pick up my calls
you never called me back
never texted
never let me know
like i was a nobody to you
like we weren't best friends
like we didn't grow up together
and i get it you're busy
but you're the one who taught me
that if you love someone enough
you'll call, you'll be there,
and i guess i'm not that person for you anymore

a white pick-up truck

the summer of 2022
you were fixing your ram 1500
you spent days and nights trying to get it fixed
when you felt like it was finally done
you started driving it
picking me up
and we went on our dates in it
there and back we drove on your white pick up
i liked it
a lot
and i told you so many times how proud of you i was
and you told me it would be my white pick-up truck whenever we got married

you broke up with me in that truck
that beautiful white 1500

months went by
yesterday
my friends took a white truck to the lake
it looked similar to yours
and on the way back from the lake
the night felt different
sitting in the passenger seat
like i used to sit in yours
looking out the window
and seeing the backend of the truck
the window rolled down as i looked at the darkness of the outside world
i went back in time
to the days it was just me and you
the late nights we spent together
just talking
driving
and listening to music
in your white pick-up truck

you said "don't look at me like that"
i respond "like what"
you said "the look of love"

that's when i knew i lost you forever

coffee gift card

you told me how much you loved the small coffee shop down the road
and i remembered it
i bought you a gift card from them today
i came home all excited, picking out what ribbon i wanted to wrap it in
i choose a silk white ribbon
and i planned on giving it to you the next time i saw you
because i know how much you love that place
how much you love those flat whites
but you didnt text me back before i got a chance
i thought it'd be a cute simple gift
something that you'd enjoy
that'd make you smile
but you didnt text me back
and you never did
now it sits on my nightstand
wrapped in the prettiest white ribbon
collecting the dust that falls from the air
that poor, unused coffee gift card
wrapped in white ribbon.

that night

yesterday i was driving to my sister's house
when i arrived
i opened the car door and as soon as i did
the outside cold
pressed against my face
i could feel goosebumps crawling up my skin
as i'm walking to her front door
i suddenly looked up and i saw the sky
the sky looked identical to that night
it brought me back
to a clear sky with stars
i'm sitting on the blanket beside you
hiding from the cold
as we both look at the stars wishing for something completely different
surrounded by silence
only you and me
yesterday i saw that night
in my memories

kids are supposed to have fun
playing with other kids
coloring

she never colored
they never let her
they never let her have friends

she never got to be a kid
and that's all she ever wanted to be

there was a time when i could come to you with any problem i was having,
and you'd sit there and help me work it out
there was a time when all your friends,
became my friends and they didn't want to talk to me because i was "pretty",
but because you convinced them that there's more to me than my appearance
there was a time when you cared
and listened
and stood up for me

yesterday i was with my guy friends
that i had to convince there's more to me than my looks
without you
and i realized i want them to stay my close guy friends
because i miss the feeling of having my brother there
i miss him listening
making me laugh
and showing me brotherly love
i miss my brother being my brother
now our relationship has completely changed,
and i try to find what it used to be
among my guy friends.

today i realized i'm going to have to think of you longer than i've even known you
you left such an impact on me
without you even knowing.

all of our memories
seemed like they'd last forever
but were gone before we could've said goodbye
in the end
was it worth knowing you for a little while
but for you to haunt me in the end?

Somebody, Nobody

romeo and juliet

you were my romeo, and i was your juliet,
but i was the only one that died in the end

haunted

i never believed in ghosts
i thought they were a lie
made up by others to scare people,
but whenever you left
your spirit
still lives within me
lingers in my thoughts
in my room
seeping into the pillows that i sleep on
i never believed in ghosts until you left
leaving me with all the memories
and no one there
leaving me haunted by the ghost of you

effortlessly

sitting in the passenger seat of your car
driving down the windy road
i look over to my left, and there you are
driving so perfectly
focusing on the road as i focus on you
i look away as the night stars catch my attention
admiring each and every one of them
later picturing that night in my memories
anywhere, anytime
i can picture that beautiful memory of us
i can picture it effortlessly

remote.

life without you is harder
and when i was with you
i could pause life
put it on hold
and unpause whenever i felt safe enough to go back
into the real world
but when you left you also paused my heart
from beating
towards everything and everyone
and i can't find the remote to unpause it

Somebody, Nobody

a year ago

a year ago i had shorter hair
i had a different car
i had different clothes
different makeup products
different daily routines
different friends
different everything
everything including where i worked
and the things i did
everything's changed
you left
when you left everything started to change
now my life is completely different from what it was a year ago
it's hard to believe because i can even see a difference in my smile
my joy
my peace
my love
my heart
from a year ago.

movies

i was walking across the grocery store
passing by the fruits, and i thought
"what if i bumped into him?"
but that doesn't happen in real life
i was driving to the gas station from work
and i thought
"what if i see him pumping up gas here"
but i realized that doesn't happen in real life
i was sitting at my favorite coffee shop
and i thought to myself
"what if he walks in, and sits right next to me?"
but this is real life
"what if you come back and stay"
but things like that don't happen in real life
only in the movies

you were the main character in my story,
but i was just a background character in yours

these days

i don't want to get out of bed
i don't want to see people
i don't want to talk
because if someone asks me how i am
i'll actually tell them the truth
i'll tell them that my eye hasn't stopped twitching for 2 weeks
i'll tell them
i haven't felt a moment of peace in a while
i'd tell them that i woke up crying this morning
i'll tell them that i just want a hug
a hug that lasts forever
a hug where i can cry on their shoulders
but i can't
because i'm scared of vulnerability
so i'm stuck in this bed
hidden from the outside cold
only coming out with a smile on my face
to people asking me how my day was
and me replying with a "great"

Somebody, Nobody

we saw each other the other day
we sat and talked for hours
remembering the past
catching up
talking about how it used to be
and how significant we were
when you decided to leave
i always kept hope
hope that one day you'd return
but im your maybe
i'm something you're not sure about
one foot in and one foot out
i think i slowly realized that im too full of life to be someones maybe
in the moment
looking at you
staring into your big blue eyes
i feel all the possibilities
but i forget my value in the rush
the potential that's wasted
on you
for a maybe.

fall leaves

i think i'm too nice
let people walk all over me like fall leaves
filling the sidewalks
roads
being trampled over
eventually disintegrating into the ground
it's harder when you're a girl
just a girl who's trying to make it in this cruel world
ruled by monsters
people who don't pick up the fallen leaves
admire the different colors
red, orange, brown
monsters who just wait for them to disintegrate
vanish
back into the earth

i bought a new car
the same car we had our first memories in
i didn't even want to buy it because of the emotional attachment i have to you
but i ended up bidding and i won
throughout the weeks that i was fixing it
all i could think about was
"oh if he could see me now"
"i have one of the cars he adores"
but i came to realize none of that matters.
sadly you wouldn't care
not about the car i drive
or the house i live in
or the friends i have
or any accomplishments i've achieved
because you don't care about me
you never truly did
so it doesn't matter
because sadly you wouldn't care either way

i was driving home one late night
i rolled down the windows
to feel the cold air seep into my car
i sunk my back into the seat warmer
the stars outside shined so bright
lighting up the road in front of me
and i was looking at the shiny stars
as a shooting star flew by
for just an instant
gone the next
i didn't even have to think about what to wish for
i automatically wished for you
you are my automatic wish

wonder

wonder what it feels like to be someone else
just for a second
all of their problems become my problems
just so i could forget about mine

forgetting sounds unpredictable

2022

everything felt like stepping into the lake on a hot summer's day
like a hot chocolate on a cold winter's evening
like the best italian pasta, freshly cooked
like smelling the spring flowers early in the morning
i loved it

now it's 2023
the lake doesn't cool me off
the hot chocolate has a bitter taste
the pasta is microwaved
and the spring flowers never got a chance to bloom
2023 feels different

words

i think we don't realize how much words hurt someone
i still remember the first time i was called "ugly" by a group of boys
the first time i was called "annoying"
the hurtful words that came from my family
the words after a heartbreak
every hurtful word becomes a wound
that you can't bandage up and heal
it's a trigger
a remark of the people that you trusted and that let you down
words become wounds
wounds leave scars
scars are forever

a part of me thinks you passed away.
suddenly my whole routine was disrupted
because you left
and you never told me where you were going
i haven't seen you since
like you passed away
but i never attended your funeral

Somebody, Nobody

i remember the way you walk
the way your hair sits to the left
i remember every soft smile you gave my way
every smile you'd hide by turning your face the other way
i remember every outfit you wore around me
how perfectly the colors coordinated together
i remember your beautiful dark brown eyes
covered by your long eyelashes
i vaguely remember the way your voice sounds like
but i remember how it sounded saying my name
i remember the first time you got distant
i remember the first time you stopped looking at me with a smile
when our conversations became more generic and less intimate
i remember when our inside jokes didn't make you laugh anymore
i remember when i missed you
terribly missed you
missed everything about you
and you didn't miss me

Feb 11

today's your birthday
you'd probably be celebrating with your girlfriend
your mom would give you a kiss and hug you
you have such a big heart
you'd probably buy her flowers
just because she raised you
i'd call you and we'd talk about silly things
id wish you the happiest of birthdays
but yet
you're gone
and none of this could ever happen
because you're gone
happy 24th birthday
to a special Gerasimchuk

-RIP Denis

memories

when you left
i remembered our relationship from the beginning to the end
a couple months had passed and i remembered only parts of the beginning and parts of the end
yesterday
you crossed my mind
and i realized i forgot almost all of our memories
the memories i cried about for days, weeks, months
the beautiful memories of you and me
that i tried so hard to hold onto
the memories that i kept thinking about
because i was terrified of ever losing and forgetting them
yesterday i realized i lost them and i lost you

a whole year after we met
im here
the same parking spot
same hair
same car
same outfit
but yet
im so different
i started writing a book
that you don't know about
i'm a full time college student
i don't work at the vet anymore
i don't feel the same
since last year
i don't feel the same because i
am not myself without you

Somebody, Nobody

my back is facing you
with a smile on my face
i wait for the surprise you have for me
3,2,1
i turn around
we're facing each other
a gun pointed right at my chest
tears swell up in my eyes
begging you not to
finger on the trigger
you say "i can't" as you shoot
right at my heart

-betrayed

you'll never know how many hours i've spent thinking about you
you'll never know the tiny gifts i bought for you
i kept in my room waiting to give them to you the next time i saw you
you'll never know how much i miss your smile
your laugh
and the thoughtful way you'd always bring me a water bottle when you'd pick me up
you'll never know how hard i cried that night
or how puffy my eyes were the next morning
you'll never know
and i won't ever tell you
because when i was wasting my thoughts on you
you weren't wasting a single thought on me

i think you were the best part of me
you made me be better
made me try harder
made me greater
and whenever you left
it felt like all the hard work i was putting in
was useless
you threw me out like an overused rag
you saw me and you didn't even spare my feelings
you just threw me in the trash
and maybe i still have some "better" in me
but i wanted so hard for you to be cheering me on
to look at me and cheer me on
be proud of me
because i didn't want to be "better" for anyone else, except you.

our song

i still remember the memory of how our song became our song
we were driving down to the city
as the warm summer air surrounded us
my hand was out the window
as my hair blew towards the backseat
driving down that busy highway
watching the sunset
not a single worry in my mind
i look over and there you were
singing our song
i joined in
we were singing in harmony
to our song
i think that was one of my favorite memories of us
from that day on
that was our song

a year later
i can't listen to that song
one of our best memories together
turned into something so painful
as little as a song

what hurts the most isn't the pictures,
the places we went to together.
it's the memories, the laughs, the love we shared
the love we'll never get back
never get to relive

the real you

i still think about you constantly
i don't tell anyone
but you exist in my head
you live
you laugh
you smile at me
you buy me my favorite flowers
you talk to me
you take care of me like you once did
we walk around
we drive past the city lights
with the windows down
but i think i like you more in my head
than in real life
in my head you'd never hurt me
but you hurt me in real life
the real you hurt me
i never want to see you in real life
because that would crush my fantasy of you
and then i'd hate you even in my fantasy.

Somebody, Nobody

every time she blinks
in pitch black, she sees you
an average person blinks 14 thousand to 19 thousand times a day
that's how many times you cross her mind
how many times she sees your face
now you're just a memory
trapped
only to be seen when it's dark

15 seconds

there was still hope for us in the air where i was
lingering
and it smelled beautiful
like i was breathing in the sun
i breathed it in every chance i got
and thought about all of the amazing things we didn't get a chance to do
and hoped we finally could

you met me at a red light
your car was behind mine
as you hopped out and ran to my open window
you looked at me for a couple of seconds
and told me those soul crushing words
"i can't"
just like that
the light turned green
and you ran back into your car
and i had no choice but to drive

i don't know how my foot hit the pedal
or how my hands held the steering wheel
i don't know how i was able to drive with the tears filling my eyes
just because of something that happened in 15 seconds
it hurt when you said those words to me
but it hurt even more when you thought i only deserved 15 seconds
only 15 seconds
at a red light

snapchat

i went to chick fil a
i didn't want any food so i got something light
i ordered a parfait
i know how much you love them
and i wanted to show you i bought one
because somehow now it's our thing
i was driving by a local coffee spot
and i know how much you like them
and i wanted to snap you a picture
maybe with the hopes you'd add it to your list
i was passing the place we had our first date
and i wanted to snap you
i wanted to snap you because i wanted to let you know that i remember
i remember all of our little details
everything that you've ever mentioned you liked
hated
every place we've been to
i wanted to show you all of it
because i care
but i couldn't
because
you left me on delivered 19 hours ago
and i've been hurt enough to know
19 hours leads to a day
a day leads to a week
and a week leads to forever

winter

whenever the seasons change from summer to winter
i see the leaves start to turn brown and fall
i feel the chilly wind that fall brings
no longer driving with my windows open
i sense the winter cold seeping in my room
in my pockets
on my pillow
and the cold seeping into my thoughts
making everything darker
more dim
making me feel more alone than ever
i think i hate winter because it make me feel alone just like you did

loss

when someone you love the most breaks your heart
you start looking at life in a different lens
you avoid long conversations about your past
about your future
you start looking away whenever someone looks at you
just so they don't catch your eyes
and you feel what you once felt with someone else
because you felt a loss bigger than any other
and you'd do anything just so you never feel that way again
so you keep your heart locked away
hidden
scared to give away the key

someone mentioned you yesterday, they asked me if I've ever heard of you
as soon as they did I felt my palms sweat
my face got hot and my cheeks get rosy
I thought of the possible things I could say
"yea, we've met a couple times," or "yea, we were in love" which felt the most true.
maybe I'd say " yea, we used to know each other"
but we both know it'd hurt me too much to say that in past tense.
I thought about our late night conversations, driving through that rundown fast
food place we loved to go to so much. I thought about the way you used to look at
me, the way your eyes would show me just how much you actually loved me. After
noticing I've been silent for an awkward amount of time, I looked up and said "no,
i've never heard of him". I played it off and we kept our conversation going without
even mentioning my hesitation to reply. In some ways I wish my response was true,
sometimes I wish I never knew you, because let's face it, the real you was possibly
the best person I ever came to know. Yet I'm stuck talking in past tense, about you
and me.

Somebody, Nobody

sometimes i hate the way my mind works
misleading in a way
i overthink about unimportant situations
i misguide myself into thinking it was important
sometimes i wish i saw myself from a third person pov
like you see me
observant
and not quite important to think too much about
maybe you'd look at me and think it was pretty the way my bangs fell into my eyes
how my smile appears as i look at my friends
how my baggy sweatshirt sits perfectly on my tiny shoulders
or how my natural laugh is a little horrendous
but maybe you'd find beauty in that
sometimes i wish i could see myself as beautiful as you see me

crash

if you asked me if i liked you
i'd say yes
i think the way you look at me
the way you care for me
the way you treat and talk to me
makes me like you
makes me wonder what it would be like to call you mine
for us to be together one day
but if you asked me if i was ready
if you asked me to be yours
i'd say i don't know
in some ways i think i'd bother you
you're so collected
calm and patient
i'm a mess
i try
i try my hardest to keep it together
but sometimes i crash
what if i crash
and it's too much for you?
what if i'm too much for you?
so i take it back
i don't know if i like you
because i don't want you getting hurt sitting in the passenger seat when i crash

we can't be friends

it was fine
effortless for the first couple of weeks
months
you picking me up
taking me on our late night coffee dates
dinner dates
late nights talking in your car
blasting music as our hands are out of the window
with the warm evening air filling the car
it was fine
effortless
but then it became a routine
you'd text me throughout the week and ask to grab a coffee on thursday
you'd leave saturdays for our fancy dinner dates
and when your replies became less frequent
and you took longer to respond
you began to disrupt our routine
then you stopped asking me if i'll be free thursdays and saturdays
but i expected you to ask
because somehow you became part of my routine
but then you disappeared
and now i have the memories of our past playing in my head
and if you ask me to hangout
grab a coffee with you
grab dinner with you
those memories
of us
will cloud my mind
and i'll place you back into the routine
into my routine
but we both know you'll just disappear again
you won't stay
you'll leave
and yet
i still hope you'll ask me to dinner
to grab a coffee
even if i don't want it to hurt when you leave
i still want you in my routine
that's why we cant be friends
because i dont think i'll ever look at you like one.
but something much more.

North Port

i remember 3 years ago
i was in Clearwater beach Florida
and you were maybe 20 miles away
i haven't seen you for a whole year
and you were visiting from Washington state
our hometown
coincidentally we were both in the same state
at the same time
only 20 miles apart
and we were considering meeting up on my last day.

a year later you died
and i never got to see you in North Port
only 40 minutes away from me.
i think that's one of my deepest regrets
not traveling 40 minutes to see you
and a year later wishing i could have

now i'm in North Port
and it's too late
you're gone
and i'm finally here again
but i'm alone
missing you Denis

Somebody, Nobody

tomorrow

tomorrow i'll see you
i'll see you and we'll have so much fun
we'll go to our restaurant
the restaurant we fell in love with
after that, we'll walk around
walk past street lights
looking at houses
and imagine which ones we would live in
we'd talk about every detail of our day
then we'd sit in the car
roll down the windows
and you'd drive me home
singing our song in the driver's seat
as i sit in the passenger's
but
tomorrow isn't real
i'll go to our restaurant by myself
walk under the streetlights by myself
and i'll drive home
listening to our song
by myself
because tomorrow never comes

just a little longer

please just sit here with me
just a little longer
sit and share a laugh
share a smile
crack a joke
just a little longer
talk with me
tell me about your day
all your plans for this week
just a little longer
because when we get out of this car
there won't be enough time
we won't be here anymore
because we don't exist
outside of this car
so please
spare me
just a little longer

Somebody, Nobody

i wish you could make me hate you
i wish you said something
did something
worthy enough to make me hate you
you leaving wasn't enough
because the way you left was in other words
perfect
gentle
kind
but soul crushing for me
even the way you left wasn't enough
for me to hate you
i wish
i wish i could hate you
but youre the one thing that never leaves my mind
my soul
a part of me
i don't think you could ever make me hate you

seeing you again

me and my friend crack jokes in the bathroom of the park
we walk out sharing a smile
in the middle of summer, the air was hot and humid
a couple of steps in front of me
you stood
the smile i had on my face quickly left my expression as we saw each other
our eyes met
that moment
everything that we were
everything we shared
all the love we had
rushed back into my memory
including the day you left
i stood there
as my stomach dropped
as my heart started racing
and my breathing became heavy
it felt like minutes
before our eyes said goodbye to each other
but it was only seconds
in that moment i saw how happy we once were
i rapidly turned around and started walking faster and faster
away from that moment.

torture

i think i torture myself on purpose
sitting in this freezing cold chair
in the brisk mid December
while i could be on the other side of the wall
ice skating with old friends
exchanging fake laughs and fake smiles
i don't know why i do this to myself
maybe it's because of the company
i don't want to interact with people who hurt me over and over again
but i still call them my "friends"
or maybe it's me
would i be happier on the other side of the wall
or sitting on this freezing chair here in silence
is it better to be with people who make you feel alone?
or to be alone?

jealous
jealous of the next person
the next person you look at
like you used to look at me

— colored eyes

you might've never realized
but i was all yours
you were my first thought waking up
and my last going to sleep
my everything

i don't have a lot of painful memories
gut wrenching memories
but the way you left, will always taunt me
every time it crosses my mind
i have to immediately think about something else
my stomach drops
blood turns cold
heart beats faster
i lose focus on everything
as my eyes start to well up with tears
as i remember those two days
in those two days
you completely broke me
shattered me

how my nails jabbed into the skin of my hands
holding my hands, wishing it wasn't real
i'll never forget feeling empty as you tried to talk to me
how you looked at me and saw nothing

Somebody, Nobody

i look over to my left and see my best friend
she's so strong
elegant and effortlessly beautiful
but she stares away with pain in her eyes
i seemed to not have noticed how you impacted her
how vulnerable
how delicate she can be
how she was with you
i saw the tears she held back
whenever she told me you left
how her strength
slowly started to diminish
just because of a selfish you
you left my best friend shattered
with tears in her eyes
tears i've never see come from her before
you, are just a boy
a boy who holds so much power
and false promises
but i will pick up where you left off
i will keep my promises
i will hold her
hug her
talk with her
and wipe away those tears you wrongfully brought her.

maybe it's all my bad luck added into one
maybe it's that one time i killed the tiny spider in my car because i was scared it might bite me
maybe it's when i didn't give the homeless person on the street the rest of my cash
maybe it's my occasional lying to my boss that i'm stuck in traffic rather than saying i slept in
maybe it's not bad luck
maybe it's just you
maybe you're the bad luck and the good luck is us not being together

i hate that i sent my condolences to my cousins after he died
even though he was my cousin too

i hate when people found out that my house burnt down
all they said was "i'm sorry"
and after a week, it was like nothing happened

i hate when i saw our mutual friend after the break up
they knew that you broke up with me
but never asked how i was doing
like they were only my friend because we were once together

i hate how you told me you loved me
made me believe you
but still ended ended up leaving

i drive with my windows down
my hand is out of the window
as i'm feeling the chilly december air grasp my fingers
the wind holds onto me
my hair swings behind me as my ears feel the cold
the stars remind me of the night we met
wherever we are in the world
we still look at the same stars
connected in some way
they shine as bright as your eyes
flickering just like diamonds
i loved looking at your diamond eyes
i look at the stars and remember yours

Somebody, Nobody

sitting in my car
listening to music
when i look over
i see your shadow
the shadow of you
sitting in my passenger seat
we don't say anything to each other
just sit in silence, listening to music
i look at the road and back at the passenger seat
and you disappear
the shadow of you disappeared like you did

out of my seat, *out of my life*

passing cars
all different colors
different models
in this big world
hoping to see yours

Somebody, Nobody

her long dark hair
lightest set of green eyes
her smile
her smile that stops the whole world
her laugh can cure any disease
her soft voice as she talks
i miss her

they run towards each other
one arm around her shoulder
the other arm on the back of her head
as she holds her tightly
their heads are tucked into each other
as they cry with joy
finally reunited
the warmth and safety they feel
couldn't be separated or expressed

she wakes up
wishing it was real.

- old friends

the sunset and stars
she was the sunset
combination of the most beautiful colors
blending together to create a stunning sky

he was the stars
filling the whole sky as he shined
lighting up the night with his beauty

the sunset would go dim
and the stars would come out
never meeting at the right time

nails

i recently started getting my nails done
my dad started paying for them
i show him and i get all excited as he smiles from my reaction
i remember when my parents were still together
my dad would never pamper my mom like he pampers me
i remember my mom telling me
how much it hurt her that he never bought her flowers
or gave her money to get her nails done
it's unbelievably confusing to understand

why my dad does all these things for me but never did them for *her*

Somebody, Nobody

i don't know how to stay focused when you're around
i pretend you're just like every other person
but my heart knows
i try to stay calm
collect my breath
but my eyes catch you when you're not looking
i watch you when you're laughing with your friends
when you're walking by i notice what you're wearing
from afar i notice your hair
the way it sits perfectly along your face
the way you laugh
i replay your laugh in slow motion
the way your shoulders move up and down
and your beautiful smile
when you're sitting alone
all i want to do is come up to you
but instead my feet stay still
because what if i come up to you and i lose myself
what if i come up to you
and we fall in love
and you leave
it's safer to admire you from afar
my eyes will keep watching you
but my feet will stay still.

Somebody, Nobody

our eyes met yesterday
you probably brushed it off like it was nothing
but to me
it was like seeing a solar eclipse
the most beautiful thing i've ever laid my eyes on
gone in an instant
not ever to return
not ever being able to experience it again

- once in a lifetime

in between

in between then and now
i know you felt something
i could see the spark in your eye
when you'd look at me from across the table
i saw your smile and heard your laugh
somewhere in between then and now
you stopped looking at me like that
there was no spark in your eyes
and your smile dimmed and your laugh became quiet
what happened?
what changed?
in between
then and now

walking, talking to someone
completely out of the blue
you show up in my mind

something as small as bread we bought together months ago
reminds me of you
out of the blue

there she is

the world's prettiest girl
wearing a beautiful dress
she's dancing
swiftly moving
as the piano plays in the background
you want to talk to her but you can't
so you just watch
every move she makes
you're scared
scared of what she has to offer
you watch her as her steps become faster with the music
like a bright moon on the darkest night, she shines
people dancing around her but she's the only one you see
the spotlight is on her
you're too terrified
suddenly the music stops
she's done dancing
you look away
pretending it never happened
pretending like you never saw her

the internet says you can fall asleep quickly next to the people you feel safe with
i remember when you slept in my arms
as soon as your head hit my arm
you instantly fell asleep
maybe you felt safe around me
maybe you were really comfortable
surrounded by blankets
i'd like to think it was because you were tired
there's no guilt that way

Glasses

growing up i wasn't a "pretty girl"
i wore glasses with a slicked back ponytail everyday
i'd get made fun of
a lot
i got called "ugly", "annoying", "toothpick"
toothpick was the worst
i heard the other ones a lot and over time they wore out on me
the summer before high school
i started wearing contacts
and styling my hair
bought some new clothes
i was still the same person
but people started treating me differently
the people who once called me ugly called me "pretty"
the people who made fun of my voice, didn't anymore
i couldn't realize why
because i was still the same person when i looked in the mirror
the popular kids wanted to be my friends
teachers were nicer to me
i got in trouble less
that's when i realized i was considered "pretty"
i liked it
it was a reward i had all along
somehow i started becoming popular
and that's when people started talking behind my back
people that didn't even know me
they've never talked to me but they always said something
i started to hate being "pretty"
people didn't want to get to know me
they never asked what my interests were
people started treating me like a doll
pretty enough to look at but never to admire
when i was bullied
at least people didn't think of me as a doll
but a human
whenever i take off my makeup
and put on my glasses
i start to miss how it used to be
sometimes i even fool myself into thinking i am one of those "pretty" girls
but i could never be
i like being the annoying girl who has interests and things to say
i like wearing glasses and having an opinion
i just wish people wouldn't treat me any differently whenever i didn't wear them.

trapped in my mind

some nights i have dreams of you
coming back
i love them
you come back and you tell me how much you missed me
you come back and never leave
we do all the things we did before
we're happy, like we once were
when i wake up
it hurts the most
because i want it to be true so bad
i can't talk about this to my friends
or anyone
i don't want to say it out loud
because then i wont stop the cycle
thinking about you on and on

so i keep you *trapped in my mind*

never spoken out loud
never real

"perfect"

i strongly dislike that word
a lot of people tell me that i look "Perfect"
but perfect doesn't exist
and people that compare me to something absolutely flawless
ideal and pure
they're lying
nobody's perfect
you could come close
but we can never be "perfect"
we fix our hair to look more "perfect"
we buy expensive clothes to make us look more "perfect"
we wear makeup to cover up our imperfections
we even change the things we say to be more "perfect"
why?
i used to do all of these things
to seem more "perfect"
now i just want to be loved for who i am
i'm funny, spontaneous
and most importantly i'm not perfect and that's okay

i remember when you would come over as kids, we would make forts out of cardboard boxes. we would stay out past dark, just to play soccer together. we'd fight about silly things and then make up the same day because we missed each other so much. we'd do chores together, get in trouble together. we would make soup outside, from the dirt and leaves we found laying around. we were best friends, spending every second together. we'd even convince people that we were twins when we both wore our glasses. i knew everything about you and you knew everything about me but somewhere along the lines we drifted apart. you started spending less time with me and more with the cool kids. i spent most of my time with my group of friends. you started having a life without me in it. now we're here, i don't even know your interests or what you did last weekend and you don't care enough to tell me. sometimes i remember how it used to be, it seems so long ago but it feels like just yesterday we were back in that house fighting like kids would. i wonder what it would've been like if you were still around, how id come into your room and sit on your bed and we'd talk about our problems and make solutions for all of them. how we'd go to the grocery store together and goof around in the isles. how it would've been if you still cared. maybe you do, but actions speak louder than words. i'll never forget when it changed, not in February when you stopped answering my calls. not in April when we'd only see each other around neutral friends. but in August. in August i needed you. more than anything. more than anyone. i needed you and you weren't there. i told you how much it hurt and you sat with me for 20 minutes and talked. that was it, we never mentioned it again. i remember when i called you last year and i told you i needed you and you drove an hour to be with me. we talked the rest of the night and you gave me the tightest hug and you spent the rest of the week spending time with me and trying to make me feel better. i remember how different it was. how we grew up and where we are now. i wish you wouldn't have changed. you never asked me how i was after you left us. it broke me. more than anyone else ever did. it still does but not in the same way. for some reason i'll always think about how it was and continue to wish it didn't change.

- in a year

Sunrises

the warmth of the sun
couldn't compare to the warmth you made me feel

- thank you

her long brown hair blowing with the wind
with her light blue jeans
and the black vans she always wears

different people but still the same
they both shared so much

her eyes sparkle in the sunlight like sapphires
green like spring leaves
blue like the ocean
you took care of her
you touched her soul without even trying

- my sunflower

you were her sunflower
she loved your bright yellow colors
the way you would stand with her during a storm

she wasn't as strong as you
her colors aren't as vibrant as yours
and she could easily fall during a storm

summer turned into fall
fall brings cold weather
maybe next year they'll be planted right next to each other
so they can grow together
be as strong as they used to be

what next year brings
she won't know
but she has to learn how to be strong
strong enough to stand on her own
blossom into her own strong sunflower

-seasonal sunflowers

A blank canvas

when i look at a painting
i admire all the colors and the painted objects
i look at the streaks of the brush
how it comes and how it goes
all corners, colors, and objects
but when i look at you
i only see the canvas
there's no color
no brush patterns
no objects
blank and white
i used to look at you and see the most amount of color
beautiful tall trees swaying in the wind
sunset colors that would surround your painting
orange, pink, yellow, purple blended into the prettiest picture
now there's nothing for me to see in you
there's no colors like how you once made me feel
no tall swinging trees
nothing
you were a painting i believed was beautiful
but in reality you were blank

it feels nice to have a crush
it feels like the first day of spring
flowers are starting to bloom
a fresh breeze hitting your face
like having your hand out of the car window
on a summer evening
smiling as they cross your mind
closing your eyes to remember how they looked

i want to have a crush on you forever
i love how you make me smile and you don't even know it

i just don't know how
how to simply forget you
stuck in my head like a repeating symphony
i know every lyric and note
as you plays in my head all day

young and dumb

doing silly things we'll never be able to do when we're older
climbing rooftops
riding scooters in the dark
dancing in the summer rain
throwing footballs in the grocery store, hoping not to get caught
falling in love with the wrong people

- i'll remember all of it

staring out of the open car window as you drive
my hair blows behind me
my hand rests outside the window, softly flowing with the wind
the stars are so bright tonight
i see them hiding in between the trees
my eyes don't look at anything else
just the stars
as they follow me home
as i blink i can still see them in my memory

- Who's your star?

healing
feels like forever
months pass by but it feels just like yesterday
healing from different things
childhood trauma
breakups
car accidents
past friendships
we all feel it
some feel it more than others
i believe God gives the strongest people
the worst wars
He knows what people can handle.

other people's trauma
no matter how little
or big
it's still their wars
their battles

- don't silence someone just because you went through something "bigger"

forgetting might be easier than remembering
but i disagree
after a while
you remember the memories through a different lens
you're not sad anymore
you're just happy you got to experience it
instead of it making you cry
it puts a smile on your face

- remembrance

me -"sorry i'm talking so much, you say something"

them -" i don't have anything to say, i'm just enjoying your presence"
* leans head on their shoulder*

i can't describe it
sitting here with you
feels like home
it'll be 1 am in the freezing cold
but i wouldn't mind
i could tell you anything
and you wouldn't look at me any different
you'd just sit there and keep listening
you love me so much that you wouldn't care
and i love you
love that doesn't break
or look at you any differently
that's me and you

Somebody, Nobody

singing a song
our voices are soft
same tone
we sing the same length
we take the same breaths
we sing about You
the one thing that makes us all alike
all the same
all sharing the same love
as we worship
Him

i believe in love
the love that makes you lose track of time
the love that makes you smile so hard your cheeks start to hurt
the love that makes you giggle at your phone in a room full of people
a love that never dies but gets stronger over time
i believe in love

human things

the indentation that's left on chairs when they hit a surface for so long
the way humans adapt
the way most of us can't stand traffic
the way our hands hold the door open for the people behind us
the way some of us talk to random strangers
the way people will slow down by your broken down car and ask if you're okay
the way people hug each other
the way we comfort people who need it from us the most
the way people smile back
the way most of us brush off the simple beauty of life

sometimes beautiful things have to come to an end
the sun sets and you have to drive home
food turns bad and you have to throw it away
people leave and you have to let them go
no matter how beautiful the sunset looks
there's always one that's even more beautiful
tomorrow

something about the beach
the beautiful sunrise colors
colliding together and covering the sky
waves coming and going
back into the sea
all of it is perfect
perfect like you
you're as breathtaking as the ocean
you're as breathtaking as the clashing colors of the sky
as beautiful as the beach

wind

i removed you as a friend today
i think it was building up
and i finally dared to do it
so i did
before i did though
i looked into our chat
just a glimpse of some of the conversations we had
i read the saved chat of me saying
"hey, hope you have a safe flight"
and the one where i said
"happy birthday again, i hope this year is the best one for you"
i remember when i sent those to you
i remember not even thinking about it
just texting it to you
telling you
i remember how deeply i felt
i didn't even have to think about it being too much, or too fast
i remember there was a time you felt the same
but just like wind
it was gone
sometimes i wish that wind would blow my way again
because it was nice to feel a breeze
but then it got cold
just like your feelings towards me
so i removed you as a friend
so you can blow your wind along the coast
hitting the sand somewhere
lifting up some tree leaves
but not anywhere near me
not anymore.

-19th birthday

a couple months ago
i didn't even want to celebrate
but now
i'm glad i did
even without you here
it's beautiful
even life without you
is beautiful

a cold early spring evening
she's wearing a black sweater and blue jeans she got from target
he's wearing a black hoodie and light washed jeans
they've never met

they made plans to come together and finally meet in real life
she was so nervous she changed her outfit 3 times
nervous and thrilled

she's finally ready
she starts driving
she's there
she walked into the gas station
looking at the time on her phone
and if he had texted her
she walks around to buy time

as she walks out, he's there
parked right next to her
she takes a deep breath as she approaches his car
she opened the car door and takes a seat
they both look at each other and smile
it felt like they've known each other their whole lives

the evening continues to be full of laughs and excitement
memories no money can buy
no laughs that could be exchanged for better

-the night we met

warm like a cup of hot chocolate in December
warm like a hug from the person you love the most
warm like you made her feel

—no hot chocolate could compare

no one could ever replace our love
just like the sun rises and sets
our love never ends

you always said you'd spend my birthday with me
i remember telling you how much i hated it
all my failed expectations every year
sad truth is that i was actually excited to possibly spend it with you
sitting on the cold sand
hearing the waves
feeling the chilly beach breeze
the sun beaming on my face
kissing my cheeks
i'm glad you're not here
i needed to be alone for this

-thanks for not being here on my special day

i didn't grow up with a perfect dad
but i know my niece did
looking at them
they're more than father and daughter
they're best friends
like something from the movies
he loves her with everything he has
and he would never do anything
to hurt her

just like in the movies

i wonder what it's like to be you
full of joy and laughter
i sit in my chair admiring how beautiful you are
how you can smile and not have intrusive thoughts
i wonder how you wake up in the morning
if you go straight to your phone or a book
maybe make yourself a cup of coffee in the most perfect mug
wearing festive pj's and comfy slippers
maybe your life isn't how i imagine it to be
maybe you wake up and look in the mirror and dislike the way you look
wearing the same shirt you wore for the past couple of days
no comfy slippers just regular socks
no coffee, just water
when i look at you i admire your beauty
the beauty you portray
the beauty you feed me

i wish i could go back to the time i fell in love
love holds the most amount of joy and sorrow
love hurts and shatters
but it's worth experiencing
all the emotions are worth experiencing
every moment was worth it
love is even worth experiencing the heartbreak

Somebody, Nobody

your eyes
they don't lie
they show me exactly how you feel
without you even saying it
i get a feeling
i always do
always will
we don't say anything
so instead we speak with silence

The way you looked at me said it all

meeting someone new
talking to someone new
laughing with someone new
making memories with someone new
means I have to forget our memories
talk, laugh, and move on from you
but i'm not sure I can ever replace you
or ever forget you
you'll always be in my heart
but someone else will be worthy enough to receive my love
someone else is better than a ghost
trapped in my memory.

the reasons why i love my mom
she never makes me do things i don't want to
she looks out for me
she calms me down
she gives me wise advice
she cries with me
she sits and talks with me
she takes care of me
she cares
but if i shared my hurt with her
she would carry it with me
she'd divide the weight of my burden
among both of us
i love how her eyes squint when she laughs
i love the way she says american words
i love when her hair is long, even though she loves it short
i love how excited she gets when she buys something on sale
i love how short she is
i love that she is the calmest, sweetest person i know
i love the way she never yells at me
i love that she always has to wear moisturizer before going to bed
i love everything about her
you might think it's because she's my mom
but that's not true
she's my best friend
and I love her more than anything and anyone
she's my two in one.

ranch

we were sitting in the restaurant
under the darkened lights
surrounded by candles
and people chattering in the near distance
just the two of us
side by side
sitting in the black booth to the side
i was thinking about getting pasta
alfredo with chicken
because i didn't want you to spend so much on dinner
but you convinced me to get a steak with you
we ordered two steaks
well done
you got asparagus on the side
while i got brussel sprouts
whenever the food came you asked for a side of a1 sauce
and ordered me one as well
i tasted it and didn't enjoy it as much as you did
i briefly mentioned that i think i'd enjoy it with ranch
the second the waiter came around
you asked for a side of the ranch.
i looked at you in disbelief
i briefly mentioned it
half jokingly
half serious
but you asked the waiter to bring some anyway
you noticed
as little as a comment about a side of ranch

i never knew how much a place can bring you peace
sitting here
surrounded by strangers
the music in the background
the sweet coffee smell
here i feel safe

-my coffee shop

more than

you were my *more than*
you were more than my friend
more than someone i talked to on a daily basis
you were more than a hi, how are you
you were an i noticed this, do you want to talk about it
you were the peace
you were the love

the *more than* in my life

but now youre *no more* than just a person

just a person and *no more*

inside we're all the same
connected in some way
in some beautiful way
all wanting to be loved
admired
appreciated
all of us share so many attributes
so why do we act as if we're so different?

i didn't fully comprehend when my sister asked me if i truly loved you
i quickly responded with an " of course"
the more that time went on
i felt different
it felt different
looking back at my past friendships and relationships
i noticed i said "i love you" to a lot of people
but i didn't actually love them
after a little while, you fit into that category
i guess i really wanted to truly love you
but i couldn't
i didn't
i'm sorry for meaningless "i love yous"

- 3 words

what i'm made for.

i finally realized why i was made
created into existence
its to make people laugh to the verge of tears
to lift people up whenever they feel like falling
to heal the broken
to comfort
to hug
to love
to admire
this world and everyone that it fills
to give more love than receive
that's what I'm made for.

and whenever i get hurt in the process
of loving
of healing others
of caring
it hurts
it tears a piece of my heart
a piece of the good
but my heart restores itself
because that's just how big it really is
and that's when i continue
continue giving other people big hearts
just like mine
because that's what I was made for.

i think it's extremely beautiful the way some people pay attention
the way some people think about the little things
the things that might not even matter to most
like walking on the outer side of the sidewalk to keep someone safe from the road
like giving the sweetest part of the watermelon away
like waiting until someone gets into their house after dropping them off
so many little things that seem unimportant
i think those things are the most important

i hope you feel love
even if it breaks you
even if it destroys you
love is worth feeling

i'm leaving to the beach
and i can't wait to swim in the clear water
for my curly hair to absorb the salty sea
for my skin to tan into a light brown
to watch the sunrise and sunset
to run across the shore
to feel everything in solitude

more than compliments.

you remind me of the color yellow.
you're like all the colors of the rainbow.
you're like Christmas, when Christmas doesn't feel like Christmas.
your smile can heal the sick.
you have such a good heart.
you're so good to be around.
you have a lovely voice.
you made me feel safe.
I see Christ in you.

somewhere
somehow
i hope you think of me as much as i think of you
i hope somehow
the power
of my thoughts of you
reach you
and we think of each other

and smile

i can't wait
'til i take you to the beach
show you the beautiful hues of the sky
orange mixed with different shades of blue
and watch as your face lights up
just like mine did
watch your eyes glisten when the sun hits them
watch you in admiration
i can't wait to share a sunrise with you.

completely different

you order asparagus as a side
while i order brussel sprouts
i stop by mcdonalds on my lunch breaks
while you stop by panera bread
i go to starbucks
while you go to a family owned cafe with much better tasting coffee
we're completely different
but we still like each others company
we still connect
we still enjoy the same entree at the restaurant
we both switch between mcdonald's and panera on occasions
we still order the same coffee, flat whites
someway, somehow
we still laugh at the same jokes
somehow we still pull towards each other for more

i was always jealous of people who had blue eyes
the way their eyes would blend in with the sky
how their eyes would sparkle like diamonds
it was truly beautiful to see blue eyes fall in love with you
they sparkled differently

cold hands

i've always had cold hands
i've always had to put them in my pockets just to keep them from freezing
but then you came around
your hands are always so warm
you'd hold mine
as we look at each other
standing in the freezing cold
looking at each other
holding hands
as you'd wait for mine to get warm
it's nice because you keep my heart warm too

Somebody, Nobody

i finally see it
i understand
why my brother chose you
chose to marry you
you take care of him in a way
only you can
Thank you.
for loving him more than i do
or ever could
thats a lot of love
and he deserves it all.

go to sleep
on my arm
rest your head
and close your eyes
as the rain hits the car window
as the outside cold creeps in
close your eyes and think of the sunset
the colors filling the sky
close your eyes
and sleep peacefully
on my shoulder
feeling safe
close your eyes and dream
a beautiful dream
and whenever you wake up
i hope you smile
and feel lifted
far away from stress
worries
i hope whenever you lean on my shoulder
and go to sleep
you find rest
and wake up with peace

i miss my dad
i miss how he used to call me princess growing up
i miss how he'd cut up all types of fruits for us before bed
apples, pears, and peaches
i miss his jokes, they always made me laugh
i miss when he was around more
now i see him every once in a while
that's when i notice he's getting older
i see how time changes someone
and how they begin to age
even when you never seem to notice it

the dark

wanna know something terrifying?
moving on.
talking, hanging out with someone new
it makes me feel so scared
so small and vulnerable
like being in the dark
i hate the dark.
not knowing what's in front of you
where to move
not to trip
moving on feels like the dark
moving on with someone who cares about you is different
they'd lean over and turn on the light, so you can see
they'd help you walk in the darkness
they'd help you with your fear of the dark
someone who cares
gentle and caring with your heart
makes walking in the dark hopeful

women

we admire people who don't even notice us
because we have the warmest hearts
we smile whenever a little baby lets us hold them
because we have a nurturing heart
we uphold and encourage someone whenever they feel down
because we have genuine hearts
women
love to take care
to nurture
to love

real friends

real friends are hard to come by
it feels like they're extinct
but it was different when i met you
i could feel your soul
how caring and gentle you are
i never thought i'd lose you
but you made me believe that there were still real friends out there
it was hard letting you go
i never wanted to
but circumstances made it so we can't be friends anymore
you were and are
the most beautiful soul i've ever found
your name smells like roses
and i will never forget you

dog bite

i got bit by a dog today
it came out of nowhere
grabbed on to my ankle with its teeth and ran off
and it scared me
terrified me
i wasn't hurt, no blood or scratches
so i played it off like it was nothing
my throat started to hurt
and my eyes started to well up with tears
i couldn't control them
she came up and asked me if i was okay
she showed sympathy in her eyes
like she feels everything i've ever cried about
like she understands
she reaches out and gives me a hug
it almost felt like she was going to cry with me
she brings me some cream for my ankle
and rubs it in herself
taking care of me
validating my feelings
whatever i was feeling
she was feeling too
it was beautiful
i felt like i shouldn't have felt that way because there was no blood
no scratches
but she made it feel like it was okay to cry
so now i'm telling you
its okay to cry
some people will make you think it's foolish to cry about small things
but its okay to feel whatever it is you feel
it's important
no matter how little it is
if there are scratches
or if there isn't
its okay to cry

there are people i met in my life
that make me want to be worse
and not better
people who make me feel angry
feel rage
feel sad
feel betrayed
people who made me feel worthless and empty
but there are also people who make me feel loved
cared for
worthy
special
they make all the rotten people feel little
not important
people who make you feel like you're not an ordinary person
everyone who touches your heart in these ways
they're special

Somebody, Nobody

your perfect small smirk
that small, soft smile you give me
fills my heart with joy
of peace
and whenever i'm with you
i feel safe
it feels like a never ending hug
whenever i'm with you
you make me feel hugged
warm and safe.

eye contact

the eye contact where you feel the love being shared
the eye contact where you're both silent
just appreciating each other
with a soft smile
sharing eye contact
sharing the love amongst each other

someone once said to me that they'd rather never feel love just to not feel heartbreak
i agreed because i've already been through heartbreak, and it didn't feel great
but the more i thought about it
i couldn't imagine life without love
even life without heartbreak
love between family members, friends
and someone special
love is the one emotion that makes you feel every other emotion
love makes you angry, envious and hopeless
but loving someone also makes you feel excitement and joy
peace, warmth, and safety
love is beautiful, even when it doesn't seem like it
it's beautiful to feel everything because you love someone so deeply
and heartbreak makes you cherish love even more

wifi

sometimes i forget i have a sister
because she's always in her own world
so often we forget to talk
we forget we exist to each other
but when we reconnect
we talk for hours and hours
about silly things
about important things
and everything in between
it's beautiful to reconnect with someone
it reassures me there's love
and there always will be
i hope me and her stay connected
whenever we're near each other
i want us to connect like wifi
instantly

somewhere

maybe it was when the sunroof was open in your car
you were taking me home after dinner
when you asked me if the cold winter air was hitting my head
and i replied with a no
but you proceeded to place your hand on the top of my head just to make sure
maybe it was when we were at the restaurant
and i briefly mentioned i think my steak would taste better with a side of ranch
and whenever the waiter came around
you asked her to bring some out
maybe it's whenever you pick me up
and i get in the car
there's already a chilly water bottle waiting for me on my side of the cupholder
maybe it's all the little things in between
opening all the doors for me
asking if i'm too cold or too hot
making the reservations without my help
buying me and my mom flowers
asking me if i'm okay.
all the little and big things that you do
made me realize
somewhere along the lines
you are healing a heart you didn't break
somewhere along the lines
i realized how special you are
i realized, i like the little things you do
somewhere along the lines
i realized, i like you

my sweet friend

i accidentally saw you the other day
you stood outside the coffee shop talking with your friend
as i saw you from afar
you walked in and ordered your caramel latte
as you scanned the room
our eyes met and we both smiled
you walked over as that smile across your face widened with every step you took
you sat down across from me
and we started catching up
you couldn't help but smile while looking at me
and i couldn't help it either
we talked about the small things that changed over the span of us not talking
sat and just talked
looking and smiling at each other
i memorized your face
every mole
how your eyelashes curved up and to the left
and how your haircut is different from the last time i saw you
and i took it all in
i took all of you in while i still could
while you were still in front of me
because i know you have to leave soon
we could never go back to that summer in june
surrounded by the perfect weather and late night talks
we couldn't go back no matter how hard we tried
so i sat there enjoying every second of you
of what was
with you
my sweet friend in the coffee shop

all day

i could sit here and talk about you all day
i could talk about the way you looked at me
the way your eyes smile when they meet mine
the way you guided me through that hallway holding my hand
while i floated behind you
the way you told me to get on the inner side of the road
or when you told me to hug your arm when we were passing by a scary guy in the city
i could sit and talk all day about the way your eyes crinkle whenever you laugh
i could sit here and talk about your contagious smile
about the way you smell like christmas candles from bath and body works
i could sit and talk about all your "little imperfections" and how i see the beauty in all of them
i could sit here
and talk about you all day

i got stood up.
my very first time making plans with someone and them leaving me in the wind
after the night slowly faded and i realized my plans were canceled
i sat in bed feeling sorry for myself
melancholy filled my room as the happiness disappeared
i realized i didn't want to go to bed sobbing on my pillow
so i walked out of my room and down the dark empty hall
seeing my moms room with the light still on
as i walked in, a smile appeared on my face
spreading to my eyes

i sat on her bed as we continued the night laughing and talking
that night i went to bed with a smile on my face
happy that i got stood up.

my sunflower

your hair glimmers as it catches the light outside the window at the coffee shop
your back is facing me
as I sit and admire the person you've become
feet away from each other but I feel your warm soul
as I look at you
I see how much you've changed
how much you've grown
the strength you've gained
I didn't say it
but i'm proud of you
of the woman you've become
of the bravery you grasped
of the hardships you've overcome
of the never endless laughs you give to people
i'm proud of the girl in the coffee shop

next to you

i was always scared of dying
the unpredictable feeling made me eerie
not knowing when and how
but i think even the scariest things in life
would be okay if i was next to you
even dying next to you
sounds perfect
kinda like a happy ending

pocket-sized problems/ reset

i went to visit family in a different state
i booked a ticket and flew across the U.S.
i didn't have much expectations before arriving
so i was really unprepared for the way i would leave
after a couple days spent with family
surrounded by different places
different roads
and meeting new people
i realized my problems back home are so pocket-sized
experiencing the beautiful unknown
making the uncomfortable moments comfortable
helped me grow
way more than expected
i left my little get away with my heart so full
with so many memorable memories that i will cherish forever
they filled up my thoughts as i had no more room for the old ones
when i arrived back home
i was eager to hug my mom
drive my car
and finally sleep in my own bed again
but driving back home from the airport
the roads that held so much awful memories for me
faded
the places i so often went to
lost their sentimental value to me
everything became new
like i had pressed a restart button
arriving back home
with problems so pocket-sized
helped me see everything as new
i'm so excited to see what new things
new people
and new places
"home" has to offer

"we"

and in the middle of all my chaos
there you were
buying me fruit tarts
opening all the doors for me
leading me
in the middle of all my worries
there you were
calming me down
giving me peace
in the middle of this busy, busy world
there you were
right in front of me
just me and you
in this busy world
there *we* were

cricket

when i was little
i remembered hearing a loud noise in my sleep
as soon as i woke up i looked over and on the pillow next to me laid a cricket
i quickly jumped out of bed screaming
and ran to my parents room
i crawled into their bed
laying in the middle of both of them
they hugged me tightly as my panic seeped out of the room
i remember wrapping my left arm around my mom's neck
and my right around my dad's
as we just laid there smiling and giggling
today, i'd say thank you to that cricket
as a kid it scared me
but today, i'd thank that cricket
i'd thank it for giving me the most beautiful memory i have of me and my parents
just simply hugging them as i fell asleep in their arms

yellow

i want to be as bright as the color yellow
as bright as the sun
or a fresh picked lemon
i want to smell like a spring dandelion
that just bloomed
or look like a daffodil
swaying in the summer air
but i don't think i can be as bright as the sun
or as fresh as a lemon
or even smell as good as a dandelion would
because i'm not just one color
i'm human
sometimes i'm blue like the midnight sky
sometimes i'm green like the trees
breathing in carbon dioxide that is giving you oxygen
and sometimes i'm all the colors at once
like a mesmerizing sunset across a field
every color
collaborating
to describe a perfect representation of what it's like to be "human"

fruit tart

we were deciding what to get for dessert
i spotted the fruit tart cake in the corner
with raspberries covering the top
we ended up getting two
one for you and one for me
i offered to pay and you quickly responded with a no
we sit down by the dramatic walls
designed in amelie's
you leave to get condiments
forks, napkins, and spoons for our coffees
you didn't make me worry about a thing
it's so refreshing
you're so refreshing
thoughtful
whenever i'm with you it's like an escape
we just sit and enjoy each others company
and the best part of our little escape
was the fruit tart you didn't finish
but let me take home
so i can continue the escape
the stress free escape
at home

routine

everyday i get up
spend time to do my makeup before work
brush my teeth, get dressed
leave for work
stay there until 6pm
after work i drive home
by then it's already dark outside
so when i get home
i do homework
make myself a cup of tea
snuggling in my jammies
but whenever you came around
my routine completely changed
i wake up with a smile on my face,
i spend all day at work
with that same smile on my face,
and even come home with a smile on my face.
the best part about you being in my new routine
is getting to see the same smile i put on your face

Somebody, Nobody

whenever my best friend leaves town
i always feel anxious
even if she's only leaving for a couple of days
it leaves me feeling alone
cold and isolated
she leaves and i'm stuck all alone in the city i grew up in
we don't hangout everyday either
but i like to know she's only a couple of miles away
she's my peace of mind

"perfect"

someone once said to me
you don't have to be perfect, to be perfect
i haven't stopped thinking about that
what if all my imperfections
actually make me "perfect"

our song

everyone is crowded around the kitchen table
people are playing music on the loudspeaker
one song after the other
i see you hiding in the corner talking to your friend
i ask my friend if i can play a song
and he passes his phone to me
when it starts to play
my eyes are already on you
when you look at me with a smile
lip syncing *our song*
in a room full of people who don't know how sentimental it is
there we were
singing *our song*
together
creating another beautiful moment, without even talking

in the end

i was talking with my friend
he was sharing how his beautiful mom passed away when he was little
he still remembers her voice
the way she looked in the morning
and her heart
he was telling me his dad remarried after
and he gained a little brother
i remember he told me
how painful it was losing a mom

but *in the end*, he gained a little brother

a best friend
i remember he told me
yes, tragedies happen
and it hurts

but there's always something beautiful *in the end.*

someone broke my heart
and it hurt
but i wrote a book
i accomplished something
a goal

so *in the end*

there is something beautiful

i guess the point of this book was so that people can realize
the sun sets and the sky darkens
but it always rises the next morning
how beautiful is it to know that no matter what happened to you today,
there's always tomorrow's sunrise

This book is written for those who are lost, like I was. Broken like I was. I promise there's a light outside of the tunnel. This world is cruel, harsh and full of people that will hurt you. Don't let those people choose who you become. God has a plan for everything and everyone. Everyone's timeline is different but in the end it all works out for the better. Romans 8:28 - " And we know that for those who love God all things work together for good, for those who are called according to his purpose."

Now that you know my story, tell me yours. I want to listen because no one listened to mine, except you.

-we'll see each other soon